Of Monitors

Poems and Stories

Aruni McShane

Hafan Books

Published by Hafan Books, 2023

ISBN 9781916044296

Hafan Books is a project of Swansea Asylum Seekers Support

All proceeds go to the charity

www.sass.wales

c/o PeoplePlus, 30 Orchard St, Swansea SA1 5AT

This book of short stories and poems is also a bright trumpet blast, announcing the arrival of someone who was clearly born to write.

Here are doomed marriages and adored monitor lizards, uneasy demons and dreadful fathers, all conjured into being in crisp and concise language, as tightly turned as a screw.

Spanning cultural difference and underlining human commonality, they weave in elements of fairy tale and magical realism even as they ponder the explosive madness of modern life, as bombs go off and lives are shattered.

Aruni McShane has an unflinching gaze. She is an author who can see an often cruel world for what it is, even as she looks penetratingly into the darknesses of the heart. Her flair for language shines through, complementing the insight and maturity on show.

Often brutally vivid and emotionally impactful, these unsettling stories and poems hold the reader in a metal grip. Once started, they simply will not let you go.

Yes, born to write. Just born to.

John Gower

minotaur	half-man, half-bull; mythical monster
monitor	one who keeps constant watch
monitor lizard	large carnivorous reptile
monster	mythical or real, fearsome beast or person

Contents

Poems

Stories

Sorrow

The women remained
always in the same place
wore a nose a ring
gifted by a man
later to nose led
now to enhance beauty.
The women remained
praying
patiently
stringing the beads of memories
hearts locked to hearth
flaming with half-forgotten desires.
They claimed nothing
baptized in the lake of sorrow
frozen.
Women what have you done for your fellows!?
You have left them no choice
but to fetch a bucket of icy water
from the lake.
Such sorrow.
It will be kept
for the next baby girl.

Only mine

I drew roses
I drew cacti
I drew little sprouting bulbs
in memory of my little ones.
Every line I drew
meant every journey I took
every hardship I went through.
Like an expert artist
no brush marks
smooth and nice.
The small figure with crooked teeth
on the canvas
was me.
It was so beautiful!
I thought.
And nobody,
nobody could say otherwise
as the canvas was black,
the only colour I used
was also black.

Insanity

At midnight all my fears come alive.
Then I creep from the bed
tip toe to the kitchen.
My angels are snuggled safe
and dreaming.
I fetch a pot of water,
wait patiently
till the water bubbles.
Then I try to catch every fear
by its tail –
slimy little bastards!
they always slip between my fingers
and scurry all over my body
bite my ears
put salt in my eyes
pinch my armpits
and throw parties on my veins.
Till dawn I chase them –
Ah ha! at last I catch
one by its sly head.
Keeping one hand on it
I slowly lift the pot,
trickle the boiling water
onto it –
what a relief
the burning feels so soothing.

A dead fish

I bought a fish
for supper
firm flesh
dreamy eyes
freshly dead
cold body
good fish
from the shopping bag
into the sink
when water touches its skin
it jumped over my head
squirmed
            once huh!
            twice huh!
            thrice huh!
like in early days of marriage
tried
            once huh!
the tongue was cut
            twice huh!
the legs were cut
            thrice huh!
the worm he put was growing bigger

Empty and troubled

I was asked to write poems
and even my neck thinks it a burden
to bear an empty head for no reason.
I was asked to write poems
in a language
which my mind couldn't use to
think what I think
and know what I know.
It ran away
sorry and out of order.
My eyes tried to help me.
They read many, many books
as I commanded them, but
nothing made sense.
I saw smoke as smoke
love as love
and pain as pain.
How can I be me?
How can I be expressive?
How can I write more beautifully, more powerfully
staying apart from my loved ones
in a land so cold and icy
where all my senses are frozen?

Forbidden fruit

Thoughts
trickling down my arm
blot the picture
that took so long to draw.
'Voluptuous emotions –
control yourself!'
I muttered.
Too late!
The harm was already done,
the picture
utterly destroyed.
My daughters were crying,
my husband was looking for
a murder weapon in the living room.
My tears tasted betrayal.
The man to whom I wrote love letters
secretively,
in the absence of my husband,
had eloped with my sister.
Lust turned out
to be a cobra with two heads.
Back to family life now
my husband won't turn me down.
After all he still needs a maid for the house,
a nanny for his children.
Or he will enjoy a family show

every Christmas
mocking me
'The whore wife who wanted more'
Or
'The whore wife betrayed by her sister' –
Dear husband,
(I tried to remake my blotted picture)
Not like his was a bar of chocolate
Or yours was a bitter gourd.
Well, it wasn't.
The pain was the same.
Yours was whipping
and his was acupuncture
pinched on wrong nerves.

At the party

On the wall my shadow was mimicking me.
Near my feet the fire of jealousy was warming me.
In a corner my husband was sipping
red wine and tasting
a red juicy apple
with his eyes.
I wasn't hungry but I was.
I had to wait
before I reach for food
as I was breast feeding our little one.
My eyes were fixed on him
and his apple.
Yet some cravings of men
don't permit them to see boundaries,
no matter how visible they are to others.
And my baby was still sipping.
A man with a suit –
a gentleman?
Yes he was man enough,
and his talk was gentle enough.
He came near me,
asked 'Still not asleep, huh?'
Unwillingly taking my eyes from my husband
I looked at the man
to answer his question.
His eyes were glued on my nipple.

I pulled my nipple out of my baby's mouth and shoved the
baby at the man.
It was sudden –
He had to thrust both hands forward.
Poor guy forgot to breathe or move,
just stood with my baby like a statue made of rocks.
I went near to my husband
and gave a smile, possibly the best I had ever given.
His eyes widened,
his mouth looked
like a rotten banana peel.
He came close and murmured into my ear
'Behave woman. Keep your breast inside your clothes'
His breath smelled of wine and whiskey,
his words were husky and toxic,
They made me forget myself.
I went near to the woman
who was licking an apple rather than eating it.
I snatched it away while her gaze lingered on my husband,
took a bite, fixed my clothes
and returned the apple to her husband.
I placed a kiss on the cheek
of the man who was clutching my child,
carefully took my baby from him.
And asked my shadow
to follow me.

To tame and cage

A beautiful pain
should slowly heal
using acupuncture.
A temporary entertainment:
vanilla ice cream with a date on top,
meant to pamper both your body and soul.
A permanent agony,
like a wound caused by burning,
will heal with time
but scars will remain forever.
A delusion:
like a compass for a woman
who doesn't know it's broken.
The reality
of detrimental pleasure:
everybody has found it,
felt it some way in this journey
but nobody could ever define it.
A conspiracy:
Brahma, the great god
made women from the foot of the male
and sent his penis to be bathed in milk and honey,
to be worshiped by women
scented in sandalwood and naphthalin.
A mockery:
the constitution of

religion asks her to serve
and men want to enslave.
Culture demands virginity.
Men demand sex before matrimony.
In the end the purity of a woman
is questioned if a drop of blood
does not stain a white bed sheet.
Woman is what
men sell and value,
value and sell,
praise and destroy.
In conclusion
Love is what men use
to tame and cage the female beasts.

Dear daughter,

When I say you are a flower
you must know
that a hand will reach
and pick you from your stem.
When I say you are a princess
you must know
that the world will expect
to place all their weight on your shoulders.
When I say you are a bird
you must know
even the winged creatures
should know the limitations
of the sky which is boundless.
When I say you are a doll
you must know
that you are not a doll
without an owner.
When I say you are my daughter
you must know
You shouldn't be the timid rabbit
like the mother you know.
When I say be like your father
you must know
you shouldn't be an aggressive zookeeper
but a Pied Piper:
let the tune of love make people follow you.

Preserving

I am an expert in my work.
Professional, respected.
It requires a steady hand,
a sharp eye.
I massage stiffening limbs
and loosen rigid muscles
then find a dry vein
and press the needle
right to the spot.
I know the secrets of the body.
I am never wrong.
For me it is not difficult
to take the juices out
and fill back with soda ash
and arsenic preservatives.
I remove impurities,
wash bodies with sandalwood and lavender,
whiten teeth, comb hair,
dress them in a suit or dress
saved for functions
important as this.
A little added colour, then
fold the clean hands neatly
and place on the chest.
All good to go.
No-one whom I dress here

in my office
ever returns.
I make them as perfect as dolls.
Their families take them back.
They sob but praise my work:
each doll packed away in a beautifully carved box.
I would smile and return home to my daughter.
She loved to run into the forest
swim in streams
hide in the clouds
on the mountain tops.
Some days it was impossible
to catch her for her bath.
She could never manage to stay still.
I would laugh
Gosh! who gave this much strength
to those tiny legs?
She would laugh back,
'You papa you!'
And now
my little girl lies here, waiting silently
for her papa to dress her.
I wash her with my tears tonight,
using my drowning heart
to cleanse her body of mud and blood.
My fingertips smooth her tangled hair.
No complaints tonight –
'Ouch papa! you're hurting me'

I never let you colour your face
and you were cross with me.
My beautiful bunny,
I used to say,
My beautiful bunny of the moon
Look at your face today.
What have you done?
Which colour would suit you the best?
Will this give you a natural blush?
I cannot bring you back.
My darling daughter
My jasmine flower
My breeze
My heart
My love
My pain
My –
I failed.
I could not preserve you.
Please
come again.

Asylum

Hunger was assuaged with
leftovers from McDonalds.
Thirst was suppressed with
the dregs left by consumers.
Mother became the donkey,
her back the baby's riding cart –
for a nipple of chocolate
she walked hours and hours.
The throbbing tooth didn't know
that help comes only
if the weak tongue agrees
to practice twisting daily.
So easy to explain, so hard to express.
Difficult to understand
the unknown people
in this unknown land
whether they grin or smile
or see our pain through our weary eyes.
Faith, the python
swallowed us in one go.
Karma was chasing us
for guilt unknown.
But the trees did blossom
in this painful cold
so I used to console my girls:
You will flourish too.

The Pearl of the Indian Ocean

Neither Sun nor Rain ever abandoned this Pearl of a Country. The smell of Jasmine and the beauty of Marigolds adorned the freshness of its Earth. Waterfalls fell from multi-green Mountains as Milk poured from Heaven.

The Prayers to Allah, the Chanting of Buddhist Gaatha, the Hymns of the Christian Choir, Sutra, Pooja drums and bells, together these made Harmony in the warm Air.

Gems gave themselves up to the Hands harvesting Paddy. The Waves brought immense Fish to the Men.

Under the shade of the Coconut tree grew the blessed Pineapple. Gardens overflowed with fruit: Mango, Mangosteen, Avocado, Anoda, Plantain, Banana, Durian, Jak fruit, Rose Apple, Papaya, Green Orange and Mandarin.

The Beauties who made Men stop and stare, they swept the roads in Patterns from Hair.

The Air was scented with Coriander, Cinnamon, Tea and Coffee, Sandalwood, Turmeric, Pepper, Nutmeg, Ginger, and roasted Cocoa beans: fine Aromas to Tickle the Nose.

The Beauty of fine Teak and Mahogany taught carpenters to perfect their Craftsmanship. Other giant Trees provided the Umbrella to protect Beings from Heat.

The crystal edges of the great Pagodas kissed the Sky with devotion. The Lakes made by the Ancient Heroes never let a Drop of Water fall from the Sky to waste.

Luxurious Mother, my beautiful Lanka, like the rich Ladies of Europe you spoiled your Children too much. The Hospitality you showed was misunderstood. Your Innocence was taken as Foolishness and now your Guests have poisoned your Children.

His pet and Lora

There are things I can't bear to look at but also can't destroy because of their sentimental value; they go into the attic. One day while I was tidying, cleaning, and searching the attic all at the same time, I came across this snapshot of my husband and his favourite pet. That photo brought back up to the surface all I had hidden, layers and layers down in my mind.

Lora was my best friend. After a long time, I can now remember that. There were years though when she was in my nightmares every day. Once they passed, I tried to suppress every memory of her. I learned to live in my present.

The picture shows my husband and his pet monitor. He is holding it carefully close to his chest. There is a gold chain around the monitor's neck. The expression on the monitor's face seems to suggest it is immensely proud of the jewellery its master gave it. My husband looks towards the camera, pink-cheeked, like a small boy who's been given a cute puppy for his 6th birthday. I took the photo with the camera which Lora gave me for my 22nd birthday. That was three months after our wedding, and I was still a virgin then.

Lora never married. She didn't believe in marriage. I thought twice before I wrote her name on the wedding invitation, because Lora always thought of marriage as an ankle shackle for women, and also because my mother spent a fortune having expensive gold-coloured handmade cards printed, and I didn't want to waste one. Lora would come, even if I simply sent a postcard.

'A hundred thousand rupees for some pieces of cardboard! Your mother should have given that money to her hard-working kitchen servant. Or she could have bought a few more days for her dying husband, and a first-class ticket to heaven one day for herself,' Lora giggled and hugged me. 'You could just have told me to come. I will definitely be there to see you as a bride.'

Lora was a Christian and I was Buddhist. She was of a low caste but belonged to a wealthy merchant family. I was of a superior caste but belonged to a middle-class family. In other words, she could wear knee length or even shorter dresses to church, while I had to drape metres of cloth to hide every inch of my body. What harmonised our two worlds was that I had rebellious thoughts about crossing the lines marked by my adults, and I admired her fashion sense, the way she talked, the way she handled boys, her whole life. Only, I didn't do anything about it. She was everything I wanted to be, but I was a coward. I was rebellious in my mind and heart, but I had a wobbly backbone. I couldn't stand up to society.

'What are you going to marry? A man? Or his status? Is it your wish? Or are you doing it because they want you to, because they think you'll miss your chance?'

'Stop mocking me Lora, you know my reasons better than anyone. I'm not forward with men like you, and I'm not as pretty as you. Even if I went to university, got a degree, a job, where would I end up? As someone's wife. Lester's not just any man. He's a distant cousin. He's a professor. He has his own bungalow and a Ferrari F40! All a woman could ask for!'

'Well, beware of professors. Some say they're eccentric, even weird.' She blew smoke rings, keeping a forced smile on the corners of her lips. 'Men are like cigarettes. Full of nicotine. But they smell sweet. Everyone knows they're poison, but people smoke anyway.' She shrugged. 'Best of luck.'

'For women like Lora, men are like toys to play with and then discard. She envies you. That's why she spouts all this rubbish rather than be happy you're getting married to such an eligible gentleman.' With Lora's and my mother's insights whirring in my head, the next day I married Lester.

After the ceremony, from the first moment I entered his house, I felt uneasy. In the vast living room, the walls were painted a dirty matt colour and covered with portraits and tapestries, most of them depicting lizards from all around the world. A vast hand-crafted chocolate-brown sofa made of teak was the only piece of furniture apart from a huge box-shaped glass-covered cage, with a big dead branch inside it and a small pond with muddy water and no plants. The cage took up almost all the space in the room. There were brass vases with no flowers in them. No bright colours were anywhere to be seen, no glamour or even cheerfulness.

'Lora was right,' I thought, 'maybe he is a mad professor.' The jewellery on my breast bounced up and down and my heartbeat rocketed as I slowly moved nearer to the glass to get a better view. I couldn't see anything peculiar. Then I caught sight of the reflection of a giant lizard crawling alongside me. My head started to spin, my body felt strange, I widened my mouth to scream, then everything turned black.

When next I opened my eyes, I found myself on a bed, still in the wedding dress.

'It was my pet, Mahi,' said Lester, standing right by the bed.

'No, no, it wasn't a dog,' I replied, 'It was more like a crocodile....'

'No, Damayanthi. It's a monitor. My pet,' he said calmly.

'Who?' I asked, confused.

'My pet, Mahi. Nobody's here but me and him, and my driver, Simon, and now you,' he said. After a pause he went on: 'My mother insisted that I should marry. I was fine on my own here. Simon does my cooking and laundry, no need to for you to worry. A village woman will be here later to help you with sweets and snacks. Rest now,' and he turned to go. Then he turned back and handed me a photo. 'This dropped out when your suitcase was opened.'

I blushed when I saw the snap of Lora and me, four years before. She was in a crimson frock and black pointed-toe stilettos. She had made me put on a short green frock of hers – well, not that short, knee length – and dark red lipstick, instead of my usual light pink. That day not a single boy whistled at Lora or gave her a flirtish look. I got all the attention. But when she took the photo I barely managed to raise my bowed head.

'Men like what they see so rarely,' Lora whispered in my ear and laughed to her heart's content.

***

After I got married, I was treated well. Fed well. I could visit my parents anytime. But for three months, Lester and I barely spoke, except for one conversation about monitors.

I didn't see him at all for the first few weeks. He got up at half past four every morning. I thought I'd meet him by getting up early too. I went to the kitchen, to prepare his breakfast. His driver Simon was already at work.

'Let me,' I said.

'Don't worry, miss, take your time. You can prepare his meals later. You're young. I'll be leaving him soon to join my parents up in heaven. Why don't you go and join him at the table? He'll be happy to see you,' Simon smiled.

'You are kind. No wonder he treats you like his father.' I returned the smile and went to join Lester.

The monitor took up most of the table. It must have been 5 feet long. Lester was reading his newspaper while stroking its head.

'Ha! There you are. Sorry I haven't seen you. I'm busy with a few projects. How's your stay here?'

The animal's smell and weird whooshing noises were too much. I sat on a distant chair and answered, 'I'm okay.'

The monitor turned its head towards me and flicked its tongue. My stomach rolled. 'I can face it,' I started to chant to myself, a mantra, over and over in my head.

Simon appeared with cups of tea smelling of cardamom and cinnamon and with a porcelain jar. He served us, then prepared to put something from the jar on the table near the lizard's head, but Lester stopped him. 'Later. Maybe the lady

29

won't like it.' Simon bowed his head and went out to the kitchen like an obedient dog.

'Monitors are carnivorous animals,' Lester explained. 'My Mahi is a *Varanus bengalensis*, quite common in Asia, the best friend of the chena farmers in dry zones in Sri Lanka and India. Forest clearings are havens for vipers and cobras. Monitors eat the snakes. They protect people. But, in return, men kill them.' He tried to suppress an angry note in his voice.

'I feed Mahi live chameleons, geckos, frogs, occasionally rat snakes. That's all I can find here. He doesn't like eggs. It would save me a fortune if he did,' he added. There was a pause.

'By the way, was that woman in the photo a friend of yours?' he asked quite casually.

'Yes, my friend Lora.' I finished my tea quickly. I needed to get out into the fresh air before I threw up. A throbbing headache lasted all day. I never joined him for breakfast again.

He always came home late and went straight to Mahi, picked it up and sat on the sofa with it, humming a song and stroking its head.

Once he knocked on my door late at night. I pretended to be asleep. I was under the sheets, shivering and sweating. After a few knocks he gave up and went away.

***

On my 22nd birthday I went to visit my mother. Simon took me in the car. Mother and I both liked the neighbours to be reminded that I'd married a rich man.

'Didn't our son-in-law come with you?' she asked even before I stepped inside.

'He's busy. It's my birthday but …', and I burst into tears.

'Don't be silly. Are you still a teenager needing to cut a cake and sing a song?' My mother misinterpreted as usual.

'No, but … we don't have any relationship. We don't even sleep together. And his pet …'

'What am I hearing? It's a woman's duty to arouse her man. He's a well-mannered boy. He was busy studying all his life. He must be shy. It's only the third month.'

I decided not to discuss Lester with my mother.

Later I made a call from the post office.

'Hello Lora. It's me, Damayanthi.'

'Hey, how are you? Why are you whispering?'

'Can I see you today?'

'This afternoon, some time. I'll come to your new home. Give me the number. I'll call you before I set off.'

'But … the phone's in the living room.'

'So what?'

'Nothing. I can't remember the number. Just come to the junction of Halawatha and take a taxi to his house. I mean ours. Please come, okay?'

'Of course, I will. Don't worry. You can always count on me. See you later.'

'Thanks.' She was the best friend anyone could ask for.

***

When I got home I was all set to welcome Lora, but she didn't appear until 4 o'clock. I ran to her and hugged her like a fearful baby.

She patted my shoulder and said, 'Don't worry, your mama is here now.'

I giggled. That was the first laugh I had had for ages.

Over tea I told her all about my miserable past weeks. She wasn't surprised or moved by anything I told her about Lester and his pet. She listened attentively but, as always, unlike my mother, she didn't try to advise me or say, 'I told you so.'

Then that day, for the first time, Lester came home early.

Lora jumped from her seat. I introduced them.

'Oh, hello there, Lester. I didn't see you properly at the wedding. Big crowd! I couldn't stay until the end. I'm not a huge fan of farewells. Or weddings.' Lora spoke casually.

Lester didn't bother to reply. He came straight to me. 'Simon says it's your birthday. So I've brought you some flowers. Happy birthday,' and he kissed my cheek.

I blushed. This was the first kiss I had ever received from any man, and the first kiss my husband had given me. I thought Lora was my lucky charm. He nodded to her and went inside without another word.

I was pleased he didn't talk to Lora. Any man could fall for Lora. Then I thought how easily one casual kiss from him turned me in his favour. I felt both guilty and relieved.

Lora picked up her handbag and was about to go when Lester came out with his pet, holding it like a newborn baby. Around its neck was the golden chain. The sight of that chain sent a pain running through my body. It was my birthday. For the monitor he bought a gold chain, for me just a bunch of white roses!

Suddenly, Lora came up close to me, hugged me tightly and whispered in my ear, 'Kill the animal!' I was sure Lester saw my eyes widen in shock. I tried to hide my amazement and returned her smile. Then she said goodbye.

The next morning, Lora rang.

'Damayanthi, is anyone...' a bout of coughing interrupted her, 'at home?'

'Are you okay?'

'Is anyone at home?' She cleared her throat.

'No. Are you okay?'

'I'm fine.' She coughed again. 'Good. Go to the gate. I've sent a parcel. Go and bring it in. I'll stay on the line.'

I left the receiver on the table and ran towards the gate. I looked for a parcel, but the only thing I could find was a little sachet. I picked it up and ran back to the phone.

'I only found a little packet.'

'Great! Now go to the kitchen. Pour half a bottle of milk into a bowl. Mix the drug into the milk. Then give it to the animal,' she told me.

'What? I can't! I can't even go near it!'

'Dami, listen. This might your only chance. Poison it.'

'He'll kill me if he finds out. He loves it more than me. Anyway, I can't go near it.' My whole body was wet with sweat. I couldn't hold the receiver properly. Every part of me was shivering.

'Listen,' Lora said. 'I should have told you earlier. I know Lester. I met his best friend Mahesh at a party. He was from Sri Lanka. He invited me to go for a weekend there. Lester went with us as well. We went on a trip to a village in the forest and met an old man, who took us to the woods and showed us …'. Just then I heard the car.

I quickly put down the phone, wiped away my tears, squashed the packet of powder into the palm of my hand and closed it into a fist as I went to my room. A moment later, Lester came into my room. I panicked. I rushed to the dressing table and started throwing things at him with one hand, not letting go of what was inside my fist. In two strides he came over to me and grabbed my hand. 'I didn't do anything, I didn't do anything,' I was saying.

'Relax. Take a seat.' I sat on the edge of the bed with him. I could smell the monitor on his breath, so I moved a little away. I opened my fist.

'Did she ask you to kill Mahi?' he asked.

I just slightly nodded my head.

'That photo of you and Lora gave me a shock. I couldn't understand how someone like you could be friends with someone like her. She's quite the opposite type of a woman to one that I would marry.'

'She's not that bad.' I weakly tried to rescue Lora's reputation.

'I met Lora through Mahesh, my best friend for a long time. He appreciated Lora's wit and how she handled men. He always used to tell me she was a "free bird". He saw something unique about her. I was so busy with my lizard research, I barely noticed her. So then Mahesh told me a story he'd heard in Sri Lanka about a deadly oil extracted from monitors. If one drop of this oil is put into someone's food or drink, after a day or two they'll start coughing blood, then a few days later they die, was the story. So we decided to go to check it out. Mahesh brought Lora along.'

I was confused. 'Did Mahesh come to our wedding? Is Lora still with him? Don't you like her seeing your friend? Is it because she's from a different caste? Oh trust me, she's such a good girl really ….' He stood up from the bed, and his hand struck my cheek like a thunder ball.

'STOP INTERRUPTING ME!'

I closed my mouth with both hands to stop the sound of my sobbing. He sighed.

'We met a very old man who told us he'd killed his own brother with this oil, to have his share of the paddy fields. Then he took us all out to the woods. A dead monitor was strung up over a clay pot with a fire beneath it. Another monitor was tied to the trunk of the same tree and forced to face the fire. It was screaming. As it screamed, the fire got hotter and hotter. The dead monitor's skin sweated a thin oil that slowly dripped into the pot, drop by drop. It took a long time and was terrible to watch. In the end, by the time the oil was ready to collect, the screaming animal had died from fear and exhaustion.'

He stopped and helped himself to a glass of water. After gulping the whole glass he started again.

'Killing monitors is prohibited in Sri Lanka, but they do it anyway. I felt such deep pity for the animals. Nearby was a huge termite mound. Monitors often lay their eggs in them. I dug into the mound with my bare hands and took the first egg I found. I brought it back. We got special authorization. After all, we were scientists.

'Simon! Bring Mahi. Don't worry, it won't bite you, unlike your crooked friend.' His red eyes made me shiver to my bones.

'The old man agreed to give Mahesh a sample of the oil, for experimental purposes. Later I saw Lora pour a few drops into a bottle. I mentioned this to Mahesh, but he didn't take it seriously. Mahesh and his mother both died a week after we returned to India. They died on the same day, the very same day the egg hatched. I named it Mahi, because I wanted my friend TO BE WITH ME FOREVER!'

He screamed in my face. I knew he was mad. I quickly closed my eyes expecting him to strike me again.

'You see, Lora's father was Mahesh's stepfather.' He sighed and called out for his pet again.

He sat looking coldly at my face. Then quite calmly he asked, 'By the way, did that woman finish the cup of tea you served her yesterday?'

Why killing me after I died?

I'm lying peacefully among lilies, white orchids, and roses, my favourites, as if nothing had happened. I don't want to remember what agitates me and troubles my new form.

Poor father. Since I left him for good, he's spent a fortune to redeem his reputation. This is his punishment for not disciplining his daughter. I'm soon to go six feet deep. I'll enjoy letting worms feast on my body, eat away my sins. Better than being bored watching the crowd pretend to be moved at my passing. Only my mother doesn't pretend, doesn't cry. Her eyes are blank. She avoids my father every time he reaches for her. Rich bastard, he always wanted a son to carry his name on into the next generation. In mother he only wanted a lifelong slave to dance to his tunes. Your life would have been less difficult if I'd been a son. Sorry. I made you a loser and you made me one.

But this is all about me, why and how I died. My lover broke my heart. So I died. Nothing much else to say, is there?

'The silly girls, even before 18 they're sleeping with men. This is how it always ends. Just look at this one. She disgraced her parents and for what? For a pleasure that lasts a moment. If it were you, my girl, I wouldn't wait till you did it to yourself, I'd cut you into a million pieces and feed you to the fishes!' says my aunty, furious with her daughter, who's done nothing. The poor girl is in shock.

All this drama because of me. How nice! My death has made me light-hearted and carefree.

But they're wrong. I didn't kill myself. I just let myself go insane. Or they killed me. Or I never lived at all.

Let's start, shall we?

My first and only lover broke my heart. He charmed me so my hunger for him became a never-ending ache. Let's call him Asmodeus. A demon? Yes, sort of.

***

The phone rang in the night. I could hear my father snoring. I always wondered how my mother could sleep next to him. He wouldn't wake up if a train drove through his ears. Liquor knocked him into never-never land and let us breathe freely. Sometimes I would wish whiskey would knock him into Lucifer's land.

But mother, all day long she toiled like a heavy working tractor, so it was no surprise her body's senses failed at night.

I rushed to the living room to pick up the receiver.

'Hello? Hello?' He sounded agitated.

'Yes, yes, I can hear you,' I whispered. 'I asked you not to call the landline. Please. My father will kill me.'

Sometimes my brain was puzzled about the decisions my heart made. I knew what my father was like. So why was I begging another male, one I hardly knew, to be vigilant about my safety? It's strange what my hormones pumped out, compelling me to fall in love with a man with the power to enslave me for the rest of my life under the name of wife. You dumb, stupid woman.

'Where's the fucking phone I gave you?'

'I hid it inside a teddy. I didn't have a chance to check it. If I don't get a high enough mark, my father says he'll hold my mother responsible. She'll get in trouble because of me.' I was gabbling, panicking. I had to end the call before anyone woke up. 'Anyway, see you tomorrow?'

There was a long pause at the other end. I already knew what was coming.

'No, I won't be able to. In fact I just got married. I mean, I had to. I'm flying to Italy with my wife tomorrow. So. You can keep the phone.'

I hung up and for the first time, I listened to what my head told me over my heart.

The next moment I was back in my room. thinking what to think. Not sad, not angry. I saw my teddy staring at me. I took a bed sheet and covered him. I sat on the floor and looked around. The room seemed to grow bigger, and I grew smaller. I leaned against the bed, pulled out a strand of my hair, put it into my mouth. I started to chew.

Every subsequent strand was a thought. I chewed the thought of missing his seductive touch on my body. Well, no. No! NO!

Think harder. That was not what I would miss most. I would miss the adrenaline rush when I got excited about planning to meet him secretly. I would miss tricking my father, who always thought he was the smart boy in our house with two women, two dumb idiots from birth. I would miss the thrill of going to the edge and breaking the rules! That scared me. I helped my head to think straight by giving it a few good bangs against the wall.

The door opened and my mother came in. She was talking to me, but I heard nothing.

I gestured at my homework. 'Just trying to sort out this equation,' and I burst into tears in her arms.

'Easy now. Maths is so hard. Settle down and go to sleep now. He'll be furious if you wake him up. Both of us will be in trouble. Try to sleep. I'll wake you up in the morning.' She kissed my forehead and left the room.

My father was right sometimes. My mother would never listen to the whole story before drawing her conclusions. Poor mother. How disappointed she was going to be when she discovered it wasn't a mathematical problem I had. She expected better than this from me. To be top of the class, to gain an "island rank" in the coming national exams. What big dreams she had – for herself! I was to be her ticket to escape her open prison.

Even now, these memories are difficult to swallow. So I tell myself what my mother used to say when she fed me her own cooking: 'Swallow! Chew! Don't think about what it is, just swallow, before I tell your father!'

***

I was the only virtuous girl in our high school clique, the only one who didn't have a boyfriend. I told myself, 'I don't need a man to dominate me.' But the disloyal little bitch inside me was growing to like tempting men. I was bleeding every month, craving for a man. It's disgusting now to think how I betrayed myself.

At first, it was the idea that I would dominate a man. A real man. I wanted a lion. Six feet tall. Masculine. At least 6 or 8 years older. Not like my father or... He was both the villain and the hero in my world. Whenever he yelled at my mother she shrank and curled up like a baby. Then he would forget the idea of beating her. In my case it was different. I liked to provoke him. He got really annoyed when I kept gazing directly into his eyes. He couldn't get enough of hitting me because I never cried. Finally, my mother would come between us to rescue me. Then he would stop. But my pain was always eased when I saw the disappointment written all over his face. Pain is an addiction. Now I understand my mother better. She always had a choice, but she made me her excuse to stay with him. Because pain can keep you high all day and make you work around the clock like a slave.

Anyway, the lion I found turned out to be a sly fox. I walked into his trap willingly. He always decided where we met and how often we met. He never came inside me. He always used to repeat, 'I won't ruin your life.' Oh, bless him! What a sweetheart he was! He didn't want me to get pregnant or even lose my virginity. I thought he was waiting for the auspicious time. That's our cultural thing you see. We consult an astrologist to get the best date and time to marry and get laid. If the woman mislays the hymen before the wedding rituals, it's a bad omen. The man who marries such a filthy soul will be doomed forever. Men are born with the license to sleep with any woman, before or even after marriage, but they definitely must be with a virgin in the *poruwa* stage of the wedding ceremony mantras and rituals.

Egotistical bastard. He wanted to entertain himself at no cost. I was 18 and naïve, to a certain extent. Other girls who knew the conventions, knew the world enough, were smart enough to use their boyfriend's credit cards to realise their own desires, like expensive perfumes, makeup, smart handbags. In time, they'd dump the men and move on with another.

My friends used to tell me, 'Have fun before they put a ring on your finger, and you get signed up for a life sentence of slavery, cooking, cleaning and babies.'

Me: 'But what if you lose your virginity?'

'Look, if your parents are worried about their reputation, they can replace the hymen, it's just a small fortune at a private hospital. You'll get a few good slaps of course. Who cares? Like every day. And no, before you ask, you won't get pregnant. This is the twenty-first century. Boys are more worried about that than we are. They don't want a scandal.

They're planning to marry some wealthy chick afterwards and get the loot from their parents.'

One told me, 'My sister came home last night and got beaten black and blue.'

'But why?' I asked.

'She's a nurse at a private hospital. You really have to work hard, not like the government hospitals. Her sister-in-law works in a government hospital, she takes at least 10 days off a month. No questions asked. And she always comes home early from night shifts. But my sister never comes home during night shifts, so my brother-in-law suspects she has a spare man on the go.' My friend sighed, taking out her lipstick.

'Can't she resign?' That's me with my big head and small brain.

'My dumb sister's always wanted to quit. But his business is rock bottom, so her job pays the bills. Now my father's kicked her out too. For wearing short dresses. And he found out, before she was married she kept some of her salary for herself instead of handing it all over to him for her dowry.' My friend started eying up a boy standing leaning against a shiny Mazda.

'So she's gone back to her in-laws?'

'No, to the hospital quarters. She rang me yesterday, said she was leaving the country next week. So I rang my brother-in-law and told him.' She was powdering her cheeks now.

'You bitch! Why do that? She's your sister. He'll kill her!' I felt a panic attack coming on. I started biting my nails.

'Are you kidding me? Why should I worry? What do you know about my sister and me? How many times I was beaten because of her? She always got better marks than me. Papa was always comparing me with her. I'm no good at studying. I'm going to end up as a housewife with some man just like hers. So what? At least I won't have to be compared to her anymore.'

'But... if she goes another country... She might have taken you with her. You two might have had a great life together.'

'She won't really. And anyway, you know, I used to go to her place for sleepovers, and my brother-in-law used to come to my room and do stuff.'

'"Stuff"? Were you sleeping with your sister's man?'

'No! He just liked to see me naked and touch my breasts.'

That was my last talk with that friend. That night, her sister jumped from the roof of the hospital building. She left a six-month-old daughter, so the parents arranged a new marriage for her brother-in-law. My former friend is busy now with a baby to look after, and she's pregnant too. They live with her old in-laws who need help to wash and dress.

'It was the sensible thing to do,' my mother told me. 'Who else would look after the poor child with the same love and

44

warmth as her sister?'

I had doubts about that. But I chose not to respond.

My mother's escape plan was me. My way out was my lover. I always thought he'd take me with him to a European country where, I'd heard, women are treated equally. I wasn't sure what to believe about that, or how he would treat me once we were there. A leopard can't change its spots, even if it changes its forest. But whatever the odds of freedom, the fact that he was working offshore first made me like him.

Meanwhile I was really scared about the coming national exam. Failure would be a terrible thing. My mother's disappointment, my father's wrath, all the relatives' mocking faces would be too much to handle. So just in case I didn't pass with flying colours, I had a plan B. I figured my father would be happy to give me away to the cheapest bidder, any bidder.

As for my lover, it wouldn't be an arranged marriage, so he would never ask for a dowry. Men in our culture sometimes refer to women as "the goods". If the woman is beautiful, they call her "a top piece of goods." If the woman is not so pretty and is thought to be slutty, they call her "*weasi*". In common language, the meaning is "dirty ass hole." In our culture, even a tin of tuna has more market value than a *weasi* woman. My father used to say, 'People sell old newspapers by the kilo to earn a rupee or two in hard times. But look at me! I'll have to use up all my hard-earned money to give away my cow for free.' He always thought I was stupid like a cow or a donkey. I was brave enough to tell him: 'In Hindu culture, a cow is a sacred animal, the dwelling of gods, father!'

***

Digging inside yourself is not a sensible plan, I know. The more you dig, the deeper you go, the more you get lost. The more you shed light on the dark corners of memories, the more you find demons. They cling to your nose and fill it with the filthy stink of used engine oil or sweaty palms that smothers you and silences you. Fangs out, they watch you with eyes that want to gobble. But since I am dead it's all right to dig. What else can I do? All memories are spinning around me. The noises I made from the day I was born till death and the voices I heard are all one cacophony in the air.

Some inexhaustible energy, a kind of meta-cognition is boosting my mind, even though I can't control or choose the remembered events happening around me. I don't revisit the events, the events revisit me. I never knew that when someone dies, that person becomes like a computer screen where many windows, many programmes are running at the same time. Everything is happening around me and inside me, as I try to enter my motionless body lying comfortably on a pure white velvet cot. Suddenly I'm in a very different place. Now I'm inside the nightmare I used to have every night after the breakup.

Whenever I tried to shut down my noisy brain-mill, the memory of him would hammer and torture me with every possible ugly thing, making me watch again and again the horror movie that aroused me with his tongue and the other

46

numerous humiliating and intimidating things which I did for him repeatedly until I thought I was going insane. He was my introduction to love and sex. I didn't know what that urge was. It was like a never-ending hunger. It was physical and mental too. The pleasure of eating the cake your mother allows you is nothing like as good as the pleasure you get when you sneak into her kitchen and gobble the hidden piece. That is beyond pleasure. Even if your mother gives you a hiding next day, who cares? Fun is when you discover what they are hiding from you, like my father's face when he pinched my mother's butt in the kitchen, thinking I wasn't watching.

It was sensational at the beginning when he touched my body and aroused my feelings. But the things he asked me to do for his pleasure became intolerable. It was not the sex I enjoyed: it was the secrecy. It was forbidden, illicit, and I was curious, inquisitive.

He had a car with tinted windows. In my friends' eyes I was lucky to have a boyfriend with a car: a transportable bedroom. He didn't risk his reputation, but mine was at stake all the time. So one day my uncle witnessed me one day talking with my boyfriend outside college. I was holding his hand to say goodbye.

That evening my mother was waiting outside under the mango tree in the courtyard. It was an ominous sign. Usually she went there to lament. The mango tree was her best friend, the one who knew all her deepest, ugliest secrets. Now, she tried to stop me from entering the house. But my father was standing right in the doorway. 'Nisha, come here.' His voice was calm, and he was addressing me by my name. I knew this couldn't be good.

I had two options: to run away or to face it. I chose to face it, encouraged by my mother's swollen cheek. The ten steps toward the house were taken as slowly as a sloth but the time I took to reach him passed in a blink of my eyes.

I thought I would surely collapse to the ground. I kept my head down. I didn't want to make him any angrier by looking him in the eye.

Interrogation began.

'Did you go to class today?'

'Yes father.'

'At what time?'

'Seven, maybe half past seven, father.'

'Were you there from the beginning till the end?'

'Yes father.' I never missed classes or left early like others. I knew how good and generous he was to allocate his hard-earned money to pay for college for a girl. He could have easily made me marry someone and got rid of me. But he chose not to. That was out of something inside him, some love, I guessed.

'At what time did you finish the class?'

'2 o'clock, father. Sorry, 3 o'clock, father.' At first, I forgot to add the hour I spent after the class.

'Then how did the uncle see you with a man at 2.30 near the college?'

I knew what was coming. I fell to the ground and started to cry. 'Sir stopped the class a little early and there was this boy who always comes and talks to me. But I have nothing to do with him, father. I swear. I haven't done anything wrong.' I said everything in one breath, crying and sobbing.

'Was he holding your hand when you were talking?'

'Yes father, only once, only today it happened.' I stopped giving excuses. I knew everything had been seen. I looked at my mother's face and saw in her eyes the utter shame and bitterness she felt. Now I could feel and see the wet edges of my white uniform dripping pee.

He rushed inside the house and brought out the heated iron, took hold of my left arm and pressed the iron against the skin. I could faintly hear him shouting, 'Next time it'll be your face!' Then I lost consciousness. When I woke up my forearm was in a dressing and my mother was sitting on the corner of my bed.

'Your father did it to scare you. The iron was not that hot. It might not even leave a big scar.' My mother admonished me, 'Don't you know that even if a man just touches you, you will get pregnant? Don't ever again make this mistake.'

'Mother, I know how women get pregnant. I'm almost 18,' I wanted to say, but I only mumbled, 'Sorry mother.'

It was the following night that my boyfriend phoned to tell me he'd married a rich woman and was leaving the country.

I wanted him in my life just because I chose him for myself. Everything else I ever had or did was chosen for me. The way I dressed, how I behaved, what subjects I studied, who I could talk to, what and how I ate, how I sat, legs down, hands on your lap. Sometimes I might prefer to keep my feet a little off the ground, but I wasn't allowed. It's good that our culture didn't enforce the correct way of breathing, because I often breathed through my mouth, which was not right.

My every move was judged at home and in the community, and any choices I tried to make were always wrong. I was told I knew nothing. Now I have proven them right and me wrong. I was bad. My choice was bad. And my decision to give up my life was not sensible, either. It was just pathetic.

***

In the days, weeks, and months that followed, I munched and munched and swallowed my pain. As my mother put many spices into the curry to make it taste better, I wanted to give my agony a taste. I scratched the walls, I picked up the dirt collected between the floor tiles and hid it under my nails, so that whenever I was alone, I could season and pickle my pain. I opened the bathroom tap and watched the water spill over from the bucket, until my mother shouted, 'Are you done?'

Then I sprinkled water on my hair to convince them I'd taken a bath. I liked my hair better when it tasted salty.

Mother soon understood that something was wrong. She came to my room. I was standing in front of the mirror, looking at my naked body, wondering why he had left me. I didn't even bother to turn and look at her. I could see her desperate, exhausted face in the mirror. I was wondering whether she was angry with me or with herself. Suddenly she started throwing books at me, then she, she collapsed onto my chair, tears flowing down her cheeks. For me? Herself? I don't know even now. She stayed in that miserable pose for some time, then came to me with a blanket, wrapped it around me, took me to the bed, and indicated that I should sit.

'Is this about that boy? Or is this about your father beating you?' she asked softly.

'No, mother, it's about me! It's about what I care about. It's about not being smart enough for university! It's about my choices. About not having any choices. It's about how I tricked my father! It's about the wrong choice I made to love a man!' My heart screamed. But none of these words found their way out of my mouth. All I could say was, 'Yes, mother.' And I saw my father standing at the door, looking at me with blank eyes.

***

Men are mysterious, baffling, bewildering, you see. Harder to swallow than pain.

I hated my father for what he did to my mother, or maybe I

51

should say I was jealous. Mother always hugged me, stroked my head, combed my hair, hid the little naughty things I did from him. She was mine. I didn't like the idea of sharing her with him, even as a teenager. According to the photo album, I was about three the last time he hugged me. Those snaps capture times when we forced a smile when there was truly little to smile about. Mirrors don't lie but a camera can twist the truth. When the camera wasn't there, he never smiled. Not at me, not at my mother. Every time he called me, I got goosebumps and my mother's heart began to race.

But then, when I saw him standing in my bedroom doorway, even though I was losing my mind I can clearly remember I saw some compassion for me in his eyes. For the first time, I had frightened him. I had made him scared of losing me. The thought made me laugh. My gaze moved away from him. I started to chew at my nails. My memories are like my hair and my nails. They are bitter and hard to chew and swallow but that's the only way I could survive. I bit off the worst bits and wound them up into a ball. That ball of filth was now inside my mouth. And I slowly gulped it down.

My mother was worried about me and my father was worried about his pride. How could he tell his relatives he had a lunatic daughter? I'm sure he was praising God as I grew quieter and less disturbed. When his friends came to the house, he asked my mother to lock the door of my room. I couldn't be bothered to bang on it. It wasn't that I'd completely lost my mind, as they assumed. I could understand what was going on around me. It's just that I wasn't bothered to be part of their drama anymore.

One day my father came to my room and beat me with his belt. He thought it would help me regain my senses. Mother assured him this wasn't the best cure and reminded him of the consequences if he beat me to death. I was all curled up on the floor, hugging my legs tightly to my chest and rocking my body back and forth. Munching new, sweet, pain strands from my head was delicious. I plucked a few near my forehead and offered them to my father. 'Want some?' He threw down his belt and left the room, slamming the door behind him. Mother gathered up what was left of my hair and put it in a band. She left the room without a word.

Pain became my new joy. I embraced my mother's addiction along with so much else of her.

When I thought about hell, I realised, that's how they'd torture me. By making me live in that same moment on and on indefinitely for all eternity. 'I'm a Buddhist for Christ's sake! Take me out of this memory this instant! Please!' I begged.

The next moment I was back at the funeral, back with my corpse. It reminded me of the day I died in the hospital bed when I thought I was hallucinating.

The man of my nightmares was kneeling down in front of me, then he came at me madly with a knife. He stabbed me, tore me, cut me from the stomach to the neck. I screamed frantically.

I opened my eyes and the pain diminished. I saw my body wide open on a table. Men and women in green masks were passing their hands in and out of me. They didn't feel my existence. No surprise there. I don't think anyone ever felt my existence. But still this was different. They couldn't even see me. A long bleak wail came from a machine, and they started to hurry. One was pushing my chest harder and harder and then they started to electrocute me.

Another seemed to be fascinated, digging inside my stomach. He was still busy when the others gave up. Finally, he pulled out from my tummy a dripping mass the size of a tennis ball and put it on a silver tray. He took the tray over to my mother. He presented her with the blood-drenched ball of fingernails and hair. Without hesitating, she picked up the pain I had swallowed for months, the seasoned memories, with her bare hand.

'Body and fundus of the stomach badly damaged by infection caused by this ball of nails and hair. Sorry, we were unable to save her,' the man in green pronounced.

Fate is a python. It is brutal. When a python swallows an animal, its body stretches, making room for its prey, which is held in the python's body for days till the snake can squeeze out all the juice and digest it. Death is never the end of all the suffering. I wish it were. But no. Fate, or perhaps faith, isn't finished with me yet. I am inside its belly, aching for everything to be over.

The next thing I saw from my dead eyes set my very soul on

fire.

A man in a black suit came into the room. He kissed the forehead of the body tenderly.

'Don't you dare touch my dead body, you son of a bitch! Don't let him!' I screamed but nobody heard. Nobody heard me. Nobody hears me.

Beauty and her Beast

Beauty is nothing without glamour. Glamour follows glory. And all together they kill the ordinary.

She always wanted to be that exceptional person in the village, didn't she? She was never ordinary. She wasn't the prettiest. Pretty girls are pretty common. But she was smart. She read books all the time. She saw the world differently, understood people differently, and felt differently about being a woman. She really thought she belonged to a new world where people wouldn't define her by her gender but by who she was and what she was capable of.

She collapsed onto the intricately designed bed and let her hands stretch leisurely above her head. 'I felt so much more comfortable in my cottage frock on the straw bed with a second-hand book,' she thought. But the beast had become a prince! The very thought of it gave her goosebumps. If she had just wanted a man, she could have married Gaston. Fool or wise, prince or common, a man is a man. That was her conclusion after reading so many books from the beast's library and from her own in the village. She had devoured books about history, biographies, all about the world. She saw how everything evolved with time, everything except men and their perspective on women. Down the generations that was always pretty much the same.

Her beast was now a prince, which would make things much

less pleasant. It meant entertaining men and women who call themselves ladies and gentlemen, very important people who rule over the commoners like her. She feared ladies and gentlemen. The ones she knew were anything but gentle. She didn't know how to fit into grand society. Underneath all the layers of the brilliantly embroidered frock she wore, she was still the same: a bookworm who lacked the courage to step out into the real world. And now this unknown future with the newly transformed prince. She shuddered.

'I wish he'd remained a beast,' she sighed. Until tonight, everything could talk to each other and to her. A book or a cupboard or teapot or mirror, all talkative. And the beast was available any moment she wanted him. But now he had left the castle to meet up with old friends and family. No time it took for the beast to become the busy prince again.

This thought made her angry. She went over to the elegant teak writing desk. 'Open the drawer please, lay out a sheet of paper, fetch the quill and the ink pot, lay them on the desk,' she requested. Then she sighed. The magic had gone. No self-laying papers for her anymore. As the village women had always told her: once people married, all the magic vanished, and the women became moody and strong enough to kill a chicken for supper.

She did indeed feel strong enough to question her father. She opened the drawer, took out the writing materials, laid them on the table, and after much effort to control her gown, she finally managed to sit in a comfortable position on the chair.

She dipped the quill in ink and started to write.

~~Dear f~~Father,

How could you? If you were my mother I'm sure you'd say, kill me, but I'll never give my daughter to a beast. Yet you did.

Do you think Beauty rhymes with bibliophile? You brought back books from different lands where you ventured alone while I had to look after my half-crazy sisters. They put all their time and effort into grooming themselves all day. They pretend to be ladies, which they are in appearance only. I was left with all the house chores and surviving lecherous men like Gaston. But thanks to you and the books I have a free mind, I demand more liberty, more life than an ordinary village girl. Now I'm lost in the world that books opened for me. The brave heroines inspire me. The queens who ruled their nations better than the kings. The frankness, the nudity, the personal space, the philosophical controversies, the poetry, all this intoxicates me. Why did you let me read books which don't reflect reality? Why didn't you teach all your daughters that beauty and grace and dressing up to impress a man would only lead straight to an attic full of cinders, sorrows, disappointment, disgrace, and horror, even if it looks on the outside like a shiny golden cage full of love and care?

She was panting. Her heart was pounding. Her face was red. She could feel the heat coming off her skin. She put the quill into the ink pot to catch her breath and turned round to look at her bed. Tonight, maybe, *their* bed. She shivered.

He had behaved like a beast before, that's why he had been turned into a beast. The beast is now redeemed by Beauty. So why does that witch want to turn him back into a beast again? The looks, the money, and the power are a very harmful combination, even in a beast transformed into a man. Now she felt angry again, even angrier than before, and returned to composing her letter.

Or did you think Beauty rhymes with besotted and bestiality? I may have read books, I may be different from other girls, I may have controversial ideas about certain cultural conventions, I may have read some appalling things about sex. But how could you send your daughter to a beast to …? You knew that a good lady witch had cursed him for what he was before. I'm pleased to inform you that, yes, the beast became a prince after I kissed him, out of nothing but compassion. All thanks to you. But don't witches know, don't you know that love and compassion are two very different things?

Father, I've seen you kiss your horse's forehead. What should I think? Are you are romantically involved with it?

I always wanted a dog as a pet. When you took me to the beast, I thought maybe a lion would be suitable. He had status, wealth, and a big library. All I thought I needed for a peaceful life. I told you I was fine with it.

What happened next? What changed your mind? Why did you bring Gaston here and start a war and get the witch involved? When the time came for you to face death, I expect your conscience made you feel guilty. You thought you wouldn't reach nirvana because of what you did to me. Father, you selfish man, you gave me to a beast in exchange for your own life. You cannot rectify it now, even if you wanted to. Because of you, I had to kiss the beast and he became a man again! A busy prince! Now he must prioritise his noble friends, his family, his state work and his royal duties. And he will force me to give birth to continue his dynasty. What will happen if every child I bear is a baby girl and never a son? How many times will I be in pain, spreading my legs to give birth until a male head appears from that tiny hole I have down there? How am I supposed to go to bed with a man I didn't fall in love with? I liked the beast. He respected me, loved me, cared for me, gave me space, and forgave me for reading books, and even for masturbating. Do you know why?

Because he was the beast, father, the beast! And not a prince!

Shaken

My little princess was lying at arm's length. After struggling for hours with much effort I managed to release one of my hands and reach out to her. I just could feel the touch of the tips of her fingers. 'Warm,' I thought. 'She's alive.' I tried to call her name but the heavy blocks of concrete were pressing my chest down. Breathing and talking at the same time was impossible. I could see her face, on and off, as beams of blue, red, and yellow light came through the gaps between the giant blocks. Her face was grey from dust and dirt and turned towards me, but still my brave little girl was smiling at me and I could see her sparkling eyes too. The moment I tried to return her smile the light went off again. I could not bear the thought of all that weight of concrete pressing on her fragile body. When I started to sob, it became more difficult to breathe. I calmed myself thinking of her, if her legs or hands were broken, I should be there to look after her. I must not die.

We were all planning to celebrate her birthday tonight. Everything was set. I was placing her unicorn cake on the dining table when I thought I felt the floor vibrating. I thought it was just my mind playing tricks. 'Mama, see my dress!' I was turning to look at her when everything went dark, the soothing background music turned into sounds of explosions and screams.

And here we are under a shattered house with shattered dreams. The sirens were too loud, but it was the sound of hope. A light came again from a passing torch. Her eyes were open and she was still looking at me. 'Good girl. Just hold on. Please don't close your eyes, not even for a moment,' I wanted to tell her.

'There's a woman here. Hurry up, men! Over here,' a man was shouting, aiming his torch right at my face.

I tried to tell them to leave me and attend to my daughter. But the words didn't come. My mouth was filled with dust. I tried to show them her using my eyes. But they could not understand. I was screaming inside.

'Wait, there's a little girl too,' someone shouted.

My heart was about to burst. 'Oh, my good man, just take her out! Take my girl out.' I wished he could hear me. What's the use of my voice now if I cannot speak?

They pulled her out from the rubble, rising like an angel out of ash. I was still layers and layers under. Who cares now? I could wait. I could sleep till they take me out. But then something felt wrong. For the first time I felt pain, here inside me, right in my heart. My vision blurred. I tried to lift my head to see her. The man who was trying to lift the blocks off me noticed. He signalled the man who was carrying her. She was lying over the man's shoulders. Her smile was there. Her eyes were open. And they were too open for too long.